DOUBLE DRAGON TROUBLE

By Kate McMullan
Cover illustration by Stephen Gilpin
Illustrated by Bill Basso

Grosset & Dunlap
An Imprint of Penguin Group (USA) Inc.

Double Dragon Trouble is doubly dedicated to
Daniel Worsham Daniel Worsham
—KM

To Joyce and Camille, my very lovely sisters-in-law
—BB

GROSSET & DUNLAP
Published by the Penguin Group
Penguin Group (USA) Inc., 375 Hudson Street, New York, New York 10014, USA
Penguin Group (Canada), 90 Eglinton Avenue East, Suite 700,
Toronto, Ontario M4P 2Y3, Canada (a division of Pearson Penguin Canada Inc.)
Penguin Books Ltd., 80 Strand, London WC2R 0RL, England
Penguin Group Ireland, 25 St. Stephen's Green, Dublin 2, Ireland
(a division of Penguin Books Ltd.)
Penguin Group (Australia), 250 Camberwell Road, Camberwell, Victoria 3124, Australia
(a division of Pearson Australia Group Pty. Ltd.)
Penguin Books India Pvt. Ltd., 11 Community Centre,
Panchsheel Park, New Delhi—110 017, India
Penguin Group (NZ), 67 Apollo Drive, Rosedale, Auckland 0632, New Zealand
(a division of Pearson New Zealand Ltd.)
Penguin Books (South Africa) (Pty.) Ltd., 24 Sturdee Avenue,
Rosebank, Johannesburg 2196, South Africa

Penguin Books Ltd., Registered Offices: 80 Strand, London WC2R 0RL, England

Cover illustration by Stephen Gilpin.

Text copyright © 2005 by Kate McMullan. Cover illustration copyright © 2012 by Penguin Group (USA) Inc. Illustrations copyright © 2005 by Bill Basso. This edition published in 2012 by Grosset & Dunlap, a division of Penguin Young Readers Group, 345 Hudson Street, New York, New York 10014. GROSSET & DUNLAP and DRAGON SLAYERS' ACADEMY are trademarks of Penguin Group (USA) Inc. Printed in the U.S.A.

Library of Congress Control Number: 2005015184

ISBN 978-0-448-43821-4   10 9 8 7 6

ALWAYS LEARNING   PEARSON

Chapter 1

Wiglaf raced up the East Tower stairs of Dragon Slayers' Academy. He zoomed down the hallway. He was giving up his lunch hour to go to Reporters' Round Table. He did not want to be late.

Wiglaf reached Sir Mort's classroom. He slowed down as he entered, trying to catch his breath. Sir Mort was stretched out with his armored feet up on his desk. Muffled snoring sounds came from behind his visor. Wiglaf tippy-toed past Sir Mort and slipped into a seat beside Angus.

"You're late, Wiglaf," said Erica. She stood in front of Sir Mort's desk, holding a quill and a clipboard.

"Sorry," said Wiglaf. "Frypot kept us late in Scrubbing Class."

"All right, reporters," said Erica. "Who has story ideas for the *DSA News*?"

"I want to write a story about my hometown, Toenail," said Torblad.

"This is a school paper, Torblad," said Erica. "We do school stories. Other ideas?"

Gwen raised her hand. "I want to write the 'Get to Know Me!' piece—on *me*," she said. "I could tell *DSA News* readers how it feels to be a very rich, very talented, and very fashionable princess."

"Fine," said Erica. "But keep it to one hundred words."

"So few?" cried Gwen. "But I—"

Erica cut her off. "More ideas?"

Janice raised her hand. "How about the Alchemy Convention?"

Erica tapped her quill thoughtfully on her cheek. "Go on," she said. "What's your angle?"

"How Mordred rented out our school for the convention," said Janice. "And how none of the alchemists made any gold."

"Only a huge mess," muttered Angus.

"That is why Scrubbing Class got out late," added Wiglaf. "We were scraping ashes off everything metal in the whole castle."

"It's your story, Janice," said Erica.

Now Wiglaf spoke up. "I want to write about the animals at DSA," he said. "And how we can take better care of them."

"You mean a story on your pig?" asked Erica.

"More about the animals no one thinks of," said Wiglaf. "There are a great many rats and spiders at DSA, and—"

"BOR-ring!" cried Erica. "I want real news! Not rats and spiders!"

Erica's shouting woke Sir Mort.

"Where's the dragon?" he cried, clattering to his feet. "I'll slay that fire-breather, or my name isn't Sir Reginald Rabbitheart."

"You must be dreaming, sir," said Erica. "Your name *isn't* Sir Reginald Rabbitheart."

"No?" said Sir Mort. "Pity."

"Your name is Sir Mort du Mort," Erica went on. "You are the faculty adviser for the school paper, *DSA News*."

"Well, then," said Sir Mort. "Carry on." He sank back into his seat. He put his helmeted head down on his desk. Soon he was snoring again.

"Who wants to write a story about our headmaster?" Erica asked her reporters. "You could find out what it's like to run a school. What does Mordred do all day?" She looked around the room. "Who wants it? Angus?"

"I wouldn't touch that story with a ten-foot pole," said Angus.

"I'll put it on the front page," coaxed Erica.

Angus shook his head.

"How about you, Wiggie?" asked Erica.

"I want to write about animals," said Wiglaf.

"Why not write it yourself, Erica?"

Erica scowled. "I am the editor-in-chief of this paper," she said. "I don't write stories. I assign them." Her face brightened. "And that's what I'm going to do. Angus! Wiglaf! I hereby assign you the story on Mordred! You'll do it together."

"No!" said Angus.

"I'm the boss," said Erica. "And I say yes."

Wiglaf knew it was no use arguing. Erica had made up her mind.

"Follow Mordred everywhere," Erica told them. "Don't let him out of your sight. Ask questions. Find out how a former mud-wrestling champ became headmaster of DSA. Write a big, exciting story!"

Wiglaf liked writing stories. He liked seeing his words in the *DSA News*. Maybe if he did an excellent job on the Mordred story, Erica would let him write his animal story for the next issue.

Five minutes later Wiglaf and Angus were on their way to the headmaster's office. Both lads carried clipboards, quills, and ink pots.

"Uncle Mordred won't let me interview him," complained Angus.

"Why not?" asked Wiglaf.

"If he sees me, he'll make me polish his boots," said Angus. "Or clean the grease spots off his tunic." He sighed. "Uncle Mordred doesn't like me much."

"But you are his nephew," said Wiglaf.

"That's the problem," said Angus. "My mother made Uncle Mordred take me."

They walked by the two suits of armor that stood on either side of the headmaster's office door.

Angus knocked on the door. "Maybe I'm not cut out to be a dragon slayer," he said as he waited. "But I would like to do a bold, brave deed and become a hero. Then Uncle Mordred would see that I belong here."

Heavy footsteps sounded on the marble floor behind them.

"It's Uncle Mordred!" cried Angus. "Quick! Hide!"

Forgetting all about bold deeds, Angus lunged for the armor to the right of the door. He lifted off its top half and jumped into the boots and leg plates. He lowered the top half of the armor onto his own top half.

"Jump into the other suit!" he called to Wiglaf from inside the armor. "Hurry!"

Wiglaf rushed to the armor. He put it on, just as Angus had done. He tried to hold very still.

The footsteps grew louder. Then they stopped. Wiglaf heard a key turn in a lock. The office door opened and slammed shut. Wiglaf heard muffled bumps. Then some clicks. And then—CREEEAK!

Soon he heard Mordred's voice saying, "Sixty-two."

CLINK!

"Sixty-three."

CLINK!

Wiglaf bet he knew what those sounds meant. Mordred had opened his safe. Now he was counting his gold.

"Sixty-four," Mordred said.

CLINK!

"Sixty-five."

CLINK!

How could he write a big, exciting story about Mordred counting his gold? Boring! An animal story would be much more thrilling.

Quick footsteps sounded from the entryway. Someone was running. Wiglaf heard shouting. He knew that voice. It was Mordred's scout, Yorick.

Yorick wore different disguises for different scouting jobs. Wiglaf peeked out from the armor. Today Yorick wore a brown furry suit with a fluffy tail. Was he supposed to be a squirrel? Or a strange sort of bear?

"My lord!" cried Yorick. "My lord!" He banged on Mordred's door.

"Hold your horses, man!" cried Mordred from inside the office.

Wiglaf heard coins clinking. A minute later, he heard the door open.

"What is it, Yorick?" Mordred boomed.

"This has your name on it, my lord," said Yorick. "I found it on the drawbridge, weighted down by a rock."

Wiglaf heard parchment rustling. Then silence.

"Blazing King Ken's britches!" shouted Mordred. "There's been a kidnapping!"

Wiglaf pressed his ear to the armor, hoping to hear more.

"Oh, no, Yorick!" cried Mordred. "A ransom note! From kidnappers! They want me to cough up my very own gold!" Then he burst into tears.

Chapter 2

A kidnapping! Wiglaf's heart began to thump. Who could have been kidnapped? A DSA student? Why else would Yorick bring the ransom note to Mordred? Now *this* was a news story!

Wiglaf strained to hear what was going on inside the headmaster's office.

Mordred spoke again, "Have you shown this note to anyone else, Yorick?"

"Oh, no, my lord," Yorick answered.

"Good!" said Mordred. "Say nothing of it. This will be our little secret, Yorick. Yours and mine. I shall reward you handsomely for your silence."

"Oh, thank you, my lord!" cried Yorick happily.

"Come with me to the kitchen," said Mordred.

The office door opened. Wiglaf heard a key turning in a lock.

"I shall reward you," said the headmaster, "with a great steaming mug of Frypot's hot chocolate."

"Oh," said Yorick, sounding far less happy now.

Their footsteps trailed off down the hall.

Wiglaf quickly struggled out of the armor. Angus did, too. He rushed over to Wiglaf.

"Did you hear that?" Angus whispered.

Wiglaf nodded. "Do you think Mordred will pay the ransom?"

"Not a chance," said Angus.

"We must find out who's been kidnapped," said Wiglaf. "We must try to help!"

"We must?" Angus didn't sound so sure.

"Maybe Mordred left the ransom note inside his office."

"Let's see." Angus jiggled the doorknob this way and that. The door opened.

Wiglaf's heart thumped with fear as he slipped into the headmaster's office. He shuddered to think what Mordred would do if he caught them snooping.

The lads searched Mordred's desk. No note. They looked between his couch cushions. And under all his many pillows. They found nothing. Wiglaf glanced into Mordred's trash bin. He saw torn pieces of parchment.

He gasped. "There it is! He ripped up the ransom note."

Wiglaf and Angus began picking parchment scraps out of the trash bin. The lads stuffed the pieces into their pockets. Then Angus grabbed more parchment from Mordred's desk. He tore it to bits and tossed them into the bin.

The lads quickly left the headmaster's office.

"Let us go up to the library to piece the note together," said Wiglaf. "Mordred will never come up there."

The lads hurried to the South Tower.

"Brother...Dave?" Wiglaf called, out of breath from running up the 427 steps to the DSA library.

There was no answer.

"Worm?" Angus called, panting loudly.

They heard not a peep from the young dragon who lived part-time in the library.

"Look," said Angus. "Brother Dave left a note on his desk."

Dear Readers:

I haveth gone to picketh up a new book order. I shall returneth soon with:

WHO SLEW SIR MORTIMER WIPPLEWART? by Howard I. Know

ALL MY FINGERS AND THUMBS by Count N. Tooten

GET OUT OF DEBT NOW by Owen U. Money

WHEN WILL TOMORROW COME? by Juan Day Soon

Brother Dave

Angus and Wiglaf emptied their pockets onto the library table. They sat down and began piecing torn edges of parchment scraps together. Soon thin black lines began to form into words: "*tonight*" and "*gold.*"

"'Tis not only words," said Angus. "There is also a map. Look."

Wiglaf put the last few pieces in place. Angus pasted them down on a second sheet of parchment with Brother Dave's library paste. They were missing a few scraps, which left holes in the note. But they had enough to read:

To Morded, Hed Master, DSA
Leeve a weell barrow pilled hi w old out side
Keep Away Mownten Cave. If the gold is not th y
tonight, you weel never see
* yur deer Magg   gain!*
* Signed,*
* The Kid Nappter*

Wiglaf stared at the spidery writing. The kidnapper had a serious spelling problem.

"Dear Mordred," he read aloud, filling in the missing letters. "Leave a wheelbarrow piled high with gold outside Keep Away Mountain Cave."

"If the gold is not there by tonight," Angus continued, "you will never see your dear Magg— again!"

"Who is Magg— ?" asked Wiglaf.

"Maggie?" said Angus.

"I do not know any Maggie," said Wiglaf. "Do you?"

Angus shook his head.

Wiglaf read the note again. He looked at the crudely drawn map below. It showed a path leading north from DSA to Keep Away Mountain. A blob about halfway between the two was labeled T.V.

"T.V.—that must be Toenail Village," said Wiglaf. "That means Keep Away Mountain

Cave is not far from here. If we walk quickly, we can reach it this afternoon."

"Why would we want to do that?" asked Angus.

"To rescue whoever has been kidnapped," said Wiglaf. "And this is big news, Angus. Think of the story we could write! Surely Erica would put it on the front page of the *DSA News*."

"But what if the kidnapper kidnaps us?" Angus shuddered at the thought.

"If you had been kidnapped, would you not want someone to come to your rescue?" asked Wiglaf.

"Of course," said Angus. "I would want someone bold and brave, like Sir Lancelot, to rescue me. Not some little pip-squeaks like us."

"Well, do you see Sir Lancelot here?" asked Wiglaf. "No. And the rescue must take place tonight."

Angus shook his head.

"Rescuing someone from a kidnapper would be a bold, brave deed," said Wiglaf.

Angus stared at his friend.

"We would be heroes," Wiglaf said.

"Angus du Pangus, a hero," Angus said dreamily. "That would show Uncle Mordred." He folded up the ransom note. "Come on, Wiglaf. We have to get to that cave!"

Chapter 3

Everyone was in afternoon classes. So no one was in the Lads' Dorm to see Wiglaf and Angus packing.

Wiglaf tossed his rope and his sword, Surekill, into his bundle. He had borrowed Erica's mini-torch and tinderbox. He did not think she would mind if he took them along. Not if he brought back a good story for *DSA News*.

Angus packed quickly. Then he slid back a stone in the wall and reached into a secret compartment. He pulled out his goodie box. Wiglaf watched eagerly as his friend filled a bag with Licorice Dice, Graham Cookies, Cocoa Cubes, Camelot Crunch Bars, Medieval

Marshmallows, Jolly Jelly Worms, Sugar-Lard Chewies, Gummy Eels, and Clotted Custard Cups.

Wiglaf hooked his water bag to his belt. Then he left a note on his pillow:

Erica,
    Angus and I are following a story for DSA News. *Do not tell Mordred that we are gone.*
Wiglaf

Minutes later, the lads were heading north on Huntsman's Path. Soon they reached Toenail. They made their way through its winding streets and at last came to the north end of the village. In the distance Wiglaf saw a high mountain peak.

"Keep Away Mountain," he said.

"Strange name for a mountain," said Angus. They started north on Goback Path. "Strange name for a path, too." He stopped in his tracks. "*Keep away. Go back.* Do you think someone's trying to tell us something?"

Wiglaf shrugged. "Maybe. But we must go on."

A bird above them chirped, "*Turnaround! Turnaround!*" Another chimed in with: "*Getoutahere! Getoutahere!*"

Wiglaf shivered. He tried to think of the birds' warning cries as rich details for the story he would write for *DSA News*. He wondered what he and Angus would find when they reached the cave. And whether two small, barely armed lads were really a match for a kidnapper.

On the future dragon slayers walked. They passed many a road sign, telling them where they might end up if they took the forks along Goback Path.

The signs said:

Wormbelly Village 2 rodlongs
East Ratswhiskers (or what's left of it) 4 rodlongs

Vulture Valley 98 rodlongs

(and not really worth the trip)

The lads stayed on the path, heading north. Now the signs changed.

Keep Away Mountain, straight ahead

Keep Away, this means you

ʄ u cn rd ths ɡ bck rt nw

Keep Away! Can we make it any plainer?

We don't want you here!

After that last sign, Angus stopped and said, "Let's go back."

"We went into the Cave of Doom," Wiglaf said. "And lived to tell about it."

"Maybe we shouldn't push our luck," said Angus.

"We shall be heroes, remember?" said Wiglaf. "Think of that."

Angus groaned. But on they went.

By afternoon they reached the foot of Keep Away Mountain. Wiglaf checked the path in front of them. It spiraled around the mountain up to a gaping black hole: Keep Away Cave.

"Do you want to rest before we start the climb?" asked Wiglaf.

"No," said Angus. "If I stop, I'll never go on."

They started up the rocky path. The mountain rose up on one side of them. On the other side was a steep drop-off. They had not gone far, when they came to a sign: *Bats are brown.*

They walked up and came to another sign: *Snakes are black.*

The next sign said: *If I were you*

On they walked until they came to: *I'd turn back.*

Angus froze in his tracks. "I'm scared."

"Me too," Wiglaf admitted, but they kept on walking. Before long, they came to another series of signs. These said:

Snakes are black,

Bats are brown,

If I were you,

I'd turn around.

They didn't turn around. But they did drop to their hands and knees to crawl up a difficult stretch. Neither lad dared look down.

At last they rounded the final curve—and found themselves facing a wall of rock.

Angus groaned. "We'll never make it!"

"Look, there are toe holes. And cracks in the rocks to grab," Wiglaf said. "We can climb it."

With Wiglaf in the lead, the lads stuck the toes of their boots into holes. They stuck their fingers into the cracks, and they climbed the rock wall. At last they reached the top and rolled onto a level grassy patch.

Wiglaf lay there for a moment, panting for breath.

"I can't believe I did that," said Angus. "This calls for some stash." He pulled his bag from his pocket. He gave Wiglaf one Jolly Jelly

Worm. Then he ate almost all the rest.

The lads hiked the short distance to the yawning hole in the mountain, Keep Away Cave. There were signs stuck on wooden posts all around the cave entrance. One read:

Whether your name is Ruthie or Rory,
Enter this cave and you'll be sorry!

Another said:

Whether your name is Helga or Howie,
Go away! And we mean nowie!

"Who do you suppose wrote these signs?" said Angus, his voice trembling.

"We must go in!" said Wiglaf. He sounded far braver than he felt. He lit Erica's mini-torch. He held it in one hand. In the other, he held his sword, Surekill. He stepped into Keep Away Cave.

"Oh, wait for me," wailed Angus. "I don't want to stay out here alone!"

Wiglaf felt Angus grab the back of his tunic. The two edged slowly past a huge boulder just inside the mouth of the cave and stepped into a dark narrow tunnel. They inched along. Wiglaf saw several narrower passages that led off the main tunnel to who knows where. The cave smelled of smoke and something rotten. They had to watch their step so as not to trip over the stalagmites sticking up from the cave floor. They had to crouch down to keep from scraping their heads on the pointy stalactites hanging down from the cave ceiling. It wasn't easy.

CLANG! Wiglaf kicked something. He aimed the torch at the floor of the cave.

"'Tis the armored boot of a knight!" cried Wiglaf.

"Look over there!" cried Angus. "A knight's glove! But where is the knight?"

Wiglaf had no answer. The boot was rusted. So was the glove. Whatever happened to this knight had happened many long years ago.

As they pressed on, they found the cave

floor littered with pieces of armor. Dented helmets. Rusty chest plates. Random bits of chain mail. A sword handle, with only the stump of a blade. Wiglaf thought it looked as if a terrible battle had taken place inside this cave.

"Listen!" whispered Angus.

Far away, Wiglaf heard clanking. And—was that a shriek? Yes! And there was another! He tightened his grip on Surekill and took another step.

The tunnel widened. Wiglaf saw a fire flickering in the distance. They kept on. As they got closer to the fire, the cave grew brighter. And the clanking and shrieking grew louder.

"Why did we come here?" whimpered Angus.

"Shhhh," cautioned Wiglaf. "We must take the kidnapper by surprise."

"But what if there's more than one?" Angus

squeaked. "What if there's a whole gang of them? What will we do?"

A sudden screech split the air.

"Zounds!" cried Wiglaf and Angus together. They threw their arms around each other and held on tight.

They waited. But all was quiet.

Clutching each other, they took one step. Then another.

Suddenly the cave floor gave way beneath their feet.

"AHHHHHHHHH!" screamed Wiglaf.

"AHHHHHHHHH!" screamed Angus.

They kept screaming as they tumbled down, down, down.

Chapter 4

HUD!

Wiglaf hit the hard, rocky bottom.

THUD!

Angus landed beside Wiglaf.

The mini-torch went out. Wiglaf blinked in the dim light. He wiggled his fingers. Shook his arms and legs. Rolled his head around. Nothing broken. He sat up and asked in a whisper, "Angus? Are you all right?"

"Uhhhh," said Angus.

Pounding feet sounded from high above. Then BOOM! BOOM! BOOM! Was someone banging a gong? Wiglaf heard whooping and shouting and shrieking. Now what?

"Angus," whispered Wiglaf. "I think maybe

we have been kidnapped, too."

"This is the end!" wailed Angus. "Bye, Wiglaf. Nice knowing you."

"Do not give up," said Wiglaf. "We may yet escape."

"Escape?" shouted a voice above them. "I don't think so."

A small daggerlike stone came zooming down into the pit. And then another. And another! Wiglaf and Angus shielded their heads with their hands as the pointy stones rained down on them.

"Ow! Ow! Ow!" cried Angus and Wiglaf.

At last the stones stopped falling.

"Are you all right, Angus?" Wiglaf asked.

Angus nodded. Then he shook his fist at the enemy above them and shouted, "You are the world's meanest kidnapper!"

A face jutted over the edge of the pit. A pair of eyes looked gleefully down at Wiglaf and Angus.

Wiglaf gasped. He had expected to see a cruel villain. But he found himself looking up at the face of a lad. A little lad! He looked about his brother Dudwin's age—six, maybe seven. The lad wore a bucket-shaped helmet, held on with a metal chin strap. Tufts of bright yellow hair stuck out from under the helmet.

"Who are you?" shouted Angus.

"None of your beeswax!" the lad shouted back. And he vanished from above them.

Wiglaf's head was spinning. What was going on? Why was this little lad shouting at them? He could make no sense of it at all.

"Have you been kidnapped?" called Wiglaf.

"Have you been kidnapped?" mimicked the lad.

Wiglaf looked up. There he was, peering down at them again. He had put on another helmet. This one had a metal nose-guard. All Wiglaf could see were his eyes and his grinning mouth. He was missing a front tooth.

Now a second head appeared beside the first. This one wore the bucket helmet. Wiglaf blinked. Zounds! There were two little lads!

Angus began shouting, "No! Oh, no! Oh, woe is us!"

"Angus! What is wrong?" cried Wiglaf.

"I wish it were a pair of demons!" cried Angus. "Anything would be better than this!"

"What!" cried Wiglaf. "Do you know these lads?"

"Yesssssss," wailed Angus. "They are my cousins, Bilge and Maggot!"

Wiglaf looked up. Bilge and Maggot stood at the edge of the pit, grinning down at them.

"Hallo, Angus!" said the lad with the bucket-shaped helmet.

"Hiya, Angus!" said the lad with the nose-guard helmet.

"Hiya." Angus sighed.

"We came to rescue you," Wiglaf called up.

"We don't want rescuing," said Bilge.

"Yeah," said Maggot. "We like it here."

"Can you help us out of this pit?" asked Wiglaf.

"We could," said Bilge. "But we won't." Then they both burst out laughing.

"See, Wiglaf?" Angus groaned. "They are horrible."

"Hey, guess what?" said Maggot. "This is a dragon's cave. And the dragon will be back soon. He'll be good and hungry."

"Your friend is too bony for the dragon to eat," said Bilge.

"Yeah," said Maggot. "But the dragon likes nice fat lads like you, Angus."

"Ha-ha," said Angus glumly. "Very funny."

"Angus is dragon candy," said Bilge. The two cracked up.

Angus sat straight up. "Speaking of candy," he said. "I'll give you some if you help us get out of here."

"What have you got?" asked Bilge.

"Jolly Jelly Worms," said Angus.

"Blaaaach!" said Bilge. "We hate Jelly Worms!"

"Yeah," said Maggot. "We like real worms."

"And bugs," said Bilge. "Nice crunchy ones."

Wiglaf felt sick to his stomach.

"I've got Medieval Marshmallows," said Angus.

ZIIIIP! A rope dangled down into the pit.

"Thank you!" Wiglaf cried. He took hold of it quickly.

"Not for you," shouted Bilge.

"Just tie on the candy," shouted Maggot.

"Nothing doing," said Angus. "You want my stash, you'll have to bring me up with it. And my friend, too."

WHISK! The rope disappeared.

"Let's eat some stash, Wiglaf," said Angus loudly. He pulled candy from his pocket. "I've got Graham Cookies, Cocoa Cubes, and a bag of Medieval Marshmallows. If we had a campfire down here, I'd toast a marshmallow."

"Mmmm," said Wiglaf.

"I'd put the toasted marshmallow on a Graham Cookie and top it with a Cocoa Cube," Angus went on. "I'd put another Graham Cookie on top and—yum!"

Not a peep came from Bilge or Maggot.

"It's called a s'more sandwich," Angus said. "Because after you eat one, you want s'more!"

ZIIIIP! The rope appeared again.

Angus grinned at Wiglaf and said, "Saved by a s'more."

Chapter 5

ngus handed the rope to Wiglaf. "After you," he said.

Wiglaf climbed up quickly, before Bilge and Maggot changed their minds. He scrambled to his feet on the cave floor.

"Thank you, lads," he said.

He saw that the twins wore old, rusty pieces of armor that were way too big for them. They rattled when they moved.

Bilge stepped up to Wiglaf and took the rope from his hand. P.U.! Wiglaf reeled backward. His own father, Fergus, smelled awful, as he did not believe in taking baths. But Bilge and Maggot *really* stank.

The twins threw the rope down to Angus.

With Wiglaf's help, they managed to haul him out of the pit. Then, with surprising speed, Angus rolled away from the twins and jumped to his feet.

"Stay away!" he called. "If you want a s'more, I'm warning you—keep your distance!"

"Aw, Cousin Angus," said Bilge. "Don't you trust us?"

"No," said Angus.

Maggot turned to Wiglaf. "You trust us, don't you?"

"I guess," said Wiglaf, trying to be agreeable.

"Mistake!" cried the twins together. They fell upon Wiglaf, knocking him to the cave floor. Wiglaf didn't have a chance to put up a fight. The next thing he knew, the twins had wrangled his arms behind his back.

"Egad!" cried Wiglaf as they tied his hands together and sat him up against the cave wall. "What are you doing?"

"You're our prisoner," said Bilge.

"Untie his hands!" said Angus. "Or I won't give you any stash!"

"Oh, yeah?" said Maggot.

"That's what you think!" said Bilge.

And they set upon Angus like a pair of hungry wolves.

"No!" cried Angus. "Stop!"

But his little cousins shoved him to the ground. They wrestled his stash out of his clutches and tied his hands behind his back. They dragged him over to the cave wall and propped him up beside Wiglaf.

"Two prisoners," said Maggot, grinning his gap-toothed smile. He tied Angus's right ankle to Wiglaf's left one.

"Ouch!" cried Angus. "Not so tight!"

Maggot pulled the rope tighter.

Then the twins began galloping around their camp fire. They whooped and roared. The stalactite daggers hanging from their belts banged on their rusty armor: BONG! BONG!

BONG!

"They're animals," muttered Angus.

"Animals," said Wiglaf, "would never behave this badly."

From where he sat, Wiglaf could see he was in a huge, round cavern. Long stalactites dripped down from the domed cave ceiling. Their drips formed squatty stalagmites on the cave floor below. Some stalactites and stalagmites had grown together to form thick pillars. A camp fire crackled in the middle of the cavern. The smoke rose upward to some unseen hole at the top of the cave. A ring of stalagmite benches circled the fire.

When the twins finished their wild dance, they squatted down beside the fire and dumped out all the marshmallows. Then they took their stalactite daggers off their belts, shoved marshmallow after Medieval Marshmallow onto them, and stuck them into the fire. The smell of flaming marshmallows filled the cave.

"You're burning them!" cried Angus. "Roast them slowly!"

"We like 'em burnt," said Bilge. He blew out the flame and pulled a blackened marshmallow off his stalactite. He popped it into his mouth. "Mmmm."

Tears welled up in Angus's eyes.

All this time, Wiglaf kept working to loosen the rope that tied his wrists.

"I want a s'more," shouted Bilge.

"Yeah!" yelled Maggot. "Me too."

The twins pawed through Angus's stash until they found the cookies and Cocoa Cubes. Wiglaf watched, amazed, as the twins began cramming cookies, chocolate cubes, and burnt marshmallows into their mouths, all at the same time.

"Ohhhh, I can't watch," said Angus, shutting his eyes. "Tell me when it's over."

The twins gobbled up all the cookies,

chocolate, and marshmallows.

Maggot opened his mouth wide: BURP!

Angus opened his eyes. "We came to rescue you," he said. "And this is the thanks we get."

Bilge opened his mouth so they could watch him chew.

"At least tell us what you're doing here," said Wiglaf.

"This cave is our hideout," said Maggot.

"Who are you hiding from?" said Angus.

"Ma said we had to go to school," said Bilge. "She wrote to Uncle Mordred and said we were coming. Then she packed us up and sent us off to DSA."

"Yeah," said Maggot. "But we didn't want to go."

"So we ran away," Bilge went on. "We found this cave. It was empty, except for all the old knights' armor and stuff. So we moved in."

"You mean you were never kidnapped?" Wiglaf asked the twins.

"Nah, we wrote that ransom note ourselves," said Maggot proudly. "We ran to DSA in the dark of night and left the note on the drawbridge, under a rock."

Wiglaf closed his eyes. This was nothing but a big prank!

"Did Uncle Mordred get the ransom note?" asked Bilge.

Angus nodded.

"Did he send you here with a wheelbarrow full of gold?" asked Maggot eagerly.

"Fat chance," said Angus. "You know Uncle Mordred. He's way too cheap to part with any of his gold."

"I told you so," said Bilge. He shoved his brother.

"So what?" shrieked Maggot. He threw a stone dagger at Bilge. Bilge dove for him, and soon the twins were rolling around on the ground, wrestling, punching, kicking, and biting each other.

Angus shook his head. "To think they're my blood relatives," he said sadly.

"Good thing they're wearing armor," said Wiglaf.

He was still trying to work his hands free from the rope around his wrists. He thought maybe it was a teeny bit looser. As he struggled, he felt the cave floor shake.

Wiglaf looked at Angus.

Angus's eyes widened. He had felt it, too.

THUD.

The twins stopped punching each other. They both had bloody noses.

"What is that?" whispered Wiglaf.

Bilge and Maggot only stared toward the tunnel.

"Sounds like a dragon," said Angus.

"A dragon?" said Bilge.

THUD, THUD.

"There's no dragon. We made it up," said Maggot. "To scare you."

A cloud of foul-smelling yellow smoke billowed out from the tunnel.

"Wanna bet?" said Angus. "We're all about to become dragon candy!"

Chapter 6

The twins looked at each other and yelled, "Run!"

"Wait!" cried Wiglaf. "Untie us!"

But Bilge and Maggot zoomed to the back of the cavern.

"We're toast," whimpered Angus.

Wiglaf clenched his teeth. He gave one last mighty yank—and his hand came free of the rope. He tossed it off and began to untie Angus.

THUD! THUD!

"Hurry!" cried Angus. "The dragon's coming closer!"

The footsteps grew louder. Another cloud of putrid yellow smoke whooshed out of the tunnel.

Wiglaf worked furiously. The twins were terrible spellers, but they sure tied good knots.

"Got it!" he cried at last. He flung the rope from Angus's wrists.

Angus and Wiglaf struggled to stand. Their ankles were still tied together, so each one threw an arm around the other's shoulder. They began walking fast—as if in a three-legged race—toward the rear of the cavern.

THUD!

"Who's messed up the cave?" said a low, growling voice. "Why, this place is a disgrace! A disaster!"

Wiglaf and Angus ducked behind the nearest pillar. Wiglaf had never heard a dragon use such big words before. He felt himself trembling with fear. Or maybe it was Angus trembling. Tied together as they were, he couldn't tell.

"There is only one way into this cave," growled the dragon. "So I know you're here.

Show yourself!"

Wiglaf heard clanking. He glanced over his shoulder. There, crouching behind a fat stalactite pillar, were Bilge and Maggot. They were giggling, which made their rusty armor clank.

Wiglaf gathered his nerve and peeked out from behind the pillar. By the flickering fire, he saw a huge red-scaled dragon. Purple ears— a she-dragon. Her bright orange eyes searched the cave. A dainty yellow crest sat atop her head. Wiglaf was surprised to see that around her long red neck she wore a double strand of pearls. In one front paw she clutched a very large red purse.

Wiglaf ducked back. A dragon with pearls and a purse? She didn't look terribly mean. But he had learned one thing about dragons: Never judge them by their looks.

"You asked for it," called the dragon. "Here I come!" The dragon's footsteps came closer

and closer to Wiglaf.

"Yikes!" he cried as the dragon's huge face appeared right in front of him.

"Zounds!" cried Angus.

"Schoolboys!" exclaimed the dragon. "I might have known."

The dragon hooked her claws neatly under their DSA tunics. She picked up Wiglaf and Angus and dangled them in front of her face. Up close, Wiglaf caught a whiff of lilac. Was the dragon wearing perfume?

"Are you knights-in-training?" the dragon asked.

"S-s-s-sort of," said Wiglaf.

The dragon sighed. "Real knights would never make such a mess inside my cave."

"Wasn't us—" Angus began.

"Wasn't us!" the twins chanted in singsong voices. Then they began snorting with laughter.

The dragon whirled around. "Who said that?"

"Who said that?" taunted the twins.

The dragon lunged toward where the snorts were coming from.

Angus and Wiglaf swung wildly from her claw.

"Can't get us!" cried the twins. They dashed out of the dragon's reach, then whirled around to face her.

"Chaaaaaarge!" cried the twins, waving their stalactite daggers.

"My stars!" exclaimed the dragon, leaping back.

Bilge and Maggot both poked their stone daggers into the dragon's back legs. They stuck her over and over.

"Ow! Ow!" the dragon cried. "Stop that, you naughty lads!"

But Bilge and Maggot didn't stop.

The dragon dropped Wiglaf and Angus down on the cave floor.

Wiglaf and Angus tried to make a run for

it. But with their ankles tied together, they only toppled down in a tangled heap.

"Nonny nonny poo poo!" Bilge and Maggot shouted at the dragon. "We're not scared of you!"

"No?" said the dragon. Twin clouds of angry black smoke puffed out of her purple ears. "I can fix that."

Wiglaf and Angus watched in horror as the dragon's yellow crest rose up on her head until it looked like a huge sail. Orange sparks shot from the dragon's eyes. Her pearls began to glow like globes of red-hot lava. She swiped at the twins with a long, hooked claw.

Bilge and Maggot dodged her and took off running. They zoomed across the cavern and into the tunnel.

The dragon opened her jaws and then spewed out a huge tongue of orange flame. WHOOSH! Then she put down her purse, dropped to all fours, and raced down the tunnel after the twins.

"We have to get this rope off," said Wiglaf. He bent over and yanked off his left boot. Angus did the same with his right. Both lads wiggled their feet out of the rope. They pulled their boots back on and jumped up.

"How do we get out of here?" cried Angus. "The tunnel is the only way out!"

"Come on!" said Wiglaf, running toward the tunnel. "If the dragon comes, we can duck into one of the side passages."

Keeping close together, Wiglaf and Angus felt their way along the damp cave wall. They had not gone far when they saw a light ahead. They heard clanking. And giggling.

Wiglaf and Angus crept up on the twins. Bilge had Erica's mini-torch and was waving it around.

"Shhhh!" cautioned Wiglaf when he reached them.

"Are you lunatics?" whispered Angus.

"Laughing and yucking it up when an angry dragon is after you? Be still!"

"Be still!" mimicked the twins.

"Why did you not run out of the cave and escape when you had the chance?" asked Wiglaf.

"Why should we?" said Bilge.

"Yeah," said Maggot. "It's our cave."

"Not really," said Angus. "That dragon will be back any minute. Come on!" He grabbed Maggot by his rusty chest plate.

"Hey!" yelled Maggot. "Cut it out!"

THUD! THUD!

Wiglaf grabbed the torch from Bilge and tamped it out.

The dragon's approaching footsteps echoed in the dark tunnel. She was heading back toward the cavern.

"Wait until she passes us," Wiglaf whispered. "Then we'll make a break for it."

The four lads huddled together. For once

Bilge and Maggot kept still.

The dragon's footsteps thundered louder and louder. She galloped past them, heading toward the cavern, and then the thuds began to fade.

Wiglaf lit the mini-torch. "Come on!" He led the way out to the tunnel. Angus was right behind him. Bilge and Maggot followed. *Why do they have to be wearing that old armor?* Wiglaf wondered. *It clanked like crazy!*

The four lads ran for the mouth of the cave.

"Daylight ahead!" cried Wiglaf at last.

"Coming through!" yelled Bilge. The twins elbowed their way past Wiglaf and Angus and sprinted ahead.

Wiglaf and Angus ran right on their heels.

"Almost...there!" panted Wiglaf.

Then something blotted out the daylight at the mouth of the cave. Something huge.

The dragon! She stood before them, blocking their way. She breathed out a long tongue of flame. WHOOSH!

"Yikes!" cried all the lads. They whirled around and started running back into the cave.

How had the dragon gotten to the mouth of the cave? Wiglaf hardly had time to wonder as he and the others zoomed through the tunnel—away from the flaming dragon. They rounded a bend and—

There she was in front of them!

WHOOSH!

"Egad!" shrieked the lads.

Once more they spun around and ran out the other way.

But no sooner had they started running than—

WHOOSH! The fire-breather was in front of them!

The lads turned and ran straight in the opposite direction. Wiglaf was confused. Was he running into the cave? Or out of it? He didn't know. He only knew he was running for his life.

WHOOSH! There she was—in front of them.

They spun around and—

WHOOSH! There she was again!

Dragon in front. Dragon in back. Wiglaf felt dizzy. Was he seeing double?

"There are two of them!" cried Angus.

"Twin dragons!" shouted Bilge and Maggot.

Wiglaf saw that it was true. Oh, no! They were really in trouble now. Double dragon trouble!

Chapter 7

Bilge's eyes grew wide. He pointed at the cave ceiling. "Cave-in!" he yelled. "DUCK!"

"My stars!" cried the dragon twins. They covered their faces with their front paws and fell to the cave floor.

Angus and Wiglaf threw their arms over their heads and hit the dirt.

But the twins squeezed past one dragon and took off running down the tunnel.

"Suckers!" Bilge and Maggot shrieked as they ran. "Suckers!"

Wiglaf scrambled to his feet. "Angus, get up!" he cried. "We can escape!"

But the dragon twins quickly leaped up.

"Don't even think about it," one dragon

snapped. She turned to the other dragon. "Those little guttersnipes ran back into our cave, Ethelred. They'll be hiding out in one of the passages. We can get them later. In the meantime, roll the boulder and seal the entrance."

"All right, sister," said the dragon Ethelred. She lumbered off toward the mouth of the cave.

"Prisoners!" said the remaining dragon to Wiglaf and Angus. "Hands up where I can see them. March!"

They raised their hands and marched in front of the dragon back to the cavern.

"Sit." The dragon motioned to the stone bench.

Wiglaf and Angus sat.

The dragon sat down opposite them. As they watched, her yellow crest shrank down until it was only a dainty ridge on top of her head. Her pearls cooled to a silvery white.

"I shan't tie you up, prisoners," said the dragon. "No point. The entrance is blocked. Nobody can get out." She looked around and sighed. "Our poor wreck of a cave!" She took a lace hankie out of her big red purse and dabbed at her eyes.

"Don't weep, Lucinda," said Ethelred, coming back into the cavern. Her crest was no longer a huge yellow sail. And her pearls no longer glowed. "I'll help tidy up."

"Thank you, sister," said Lucinda. "But first let us have a talk with these intruders."

Ethelred sat down beside Lucinda, facing Wiglaf and Angus.

"Our family has dwelt in this cave for seven centuries," Lucinda told them. "In all that time, not one of our ancestors ever broke a stalactite or a stalagmite."

"Now half of them are stumps!" said Ethelred sadly. "It will take years of dripping for them to grow back to their former beautiful shapes. What a pity!"

"Our great-granddaddy started a collection of antique armor," Ethelred said. "He found priceless, one-of-a-kind items. We add to it as best we can. And we display our finds on the natural ledges all over the cave."

"Now most of our precious armor has been knocked onto the floor," sniffed Lucinda. "Broken and dented! And those two little pip-squeaks are wearing the rest of it! Oh, it is just too much to bear."

"We are sorry your cave got wrecked," said Wiglaf.

"But we didn't wreck it," said Angus. "It was those other two. Here's what happened." And he told the dragon twins about Mordred and the ransom note.

"We had no idea it was a fake," added Wiglaf. "We thought we were coming on a rescue mission."

"Bilge and Maggot say this is their cave

now," Angus added. "They don't want to leave it."

Lucinda shook her large red head.

"The nerve!" she exclaimed. "One weekend at the East Armpitsia Antiques Fair—and we come back to find that our cave has been snatched!"

Wiglaf heard running footsteps. "Shhh!" he said. "Listen."

Angus and the dragons held still.

The footsteps grew louder, and Bilge and Maggot sprang out of the tunnel. They burst into the cavern, waving what looked like moldy cabbages over their heads.

"Get out of our cave!" shouted Bilge.

"My stars!" exclaimed Lucinda.

"Good grief!" cried Ethelred.

"Get out now!" cried Maggot. He tossed a piece of parchment onto the cave floor. "Or we'll give you more of *this*!"

The lads slammed their cabbagelike balls

onto the cave floor. The crash split them open. Out flew old bones, bat doo, snake heads, and moldy garbage.

Wiglaf clapped a hand over his nose. Oooh, it smelled *awful*.

Bilge and Maggot ran back into the tunnel, laughing and shouting: "Gotcha with a stink bomb! Stink bomb! Stink bomb!"

Ewwwww! Wiglaf could hardly breathe.

Ethelred and Lucinda held lacy hankies over their noses as they swept the mess into a trash bin.

"It takes forever to get bad smells out of a cave," Lucinda said. She began spraying the air with something in a bottle. "There just isn't enough air."

Wiglaf sniffed. The spray smelled sweet, like lilac. But it didn't really get rid of the stink.

Angus picked up the piece of parchment that Maggot had tossed. He read:

Git out of are cave! And we meen now!

*Ef you don git out in a our, we will reelly reck
this plac!*

Signed,

Bilge and Maggot

"Good heavens!" cried Lucinda. "Whatever
happened to being scared of dragons?

"Whatever happened to correct spelling?"
muttered Ethelred.

Something crashed in the distance.

"Oh!" cried Ethelred. "They aren't even
waiting for an answer. They're wrecking the
cave already!"

"Ethel and I are old dragons," said Lucinda,
shaking her head. "This is our retirement
cave." She glanced at her sister. "Whatever
will we do if we can't get rid of those little
whippersnappers?" She waved a paw in front
of her snout. "Oh, it still stinks in here."

"I can't stand the smell, either," Ethelred said. "We all need a breath of fresh air." She picked up her big red purse. "Come!"

Wiglaf glanced at Angus. They were leaving the cave. Maybe they could escape! And yet he felt sorry for the dragon twins. Part of him wanted to stick around and help them get rid of Bilge and Maggot.

Lucinda reached for her purse, too. She stood up. She touched her pearls with a front paw. Every single pearl in the double strand began to glow. It wasn't the scary red-hot lava glow. It was a bright white glow to light their way down the dark tunnel. "Follow me," she said. And she led the way out of the cavern.

Chapter 8

iglaf and Angus followed the dragons.
Where are Bilge and Maggot? Wiglaf wondered.
They were very quiet. Too quiet.

At last, by the shine of pearl light, Wiglaf
saw the boulder lodged in the mouth of the
cave. Ethelred picked up a long iron rod
leaning against the cave wall. She wedged
it between the rock and the cave entrance,
gritted her fangs, and gave the rod a shove.
The boulder rolled back into the cave, creating
an opening.

Lucinda, Ethelred, Wiglaf, and Angus ran
outside.

Wiglaf took a deep breath. Ahhh! The fresh
air smelled sweet after the stinky cave. It was

cool outside. The sun was just going down. A full moon was on the rise.

Lucinda and Ethelred gulped the fresh air loudly. Then they stretched—lengthening their long, scaly red necks and spreading out their wings.

"Ah!" exclaimed Ethelred. "I feel better already."

"I do, too," said Wiglaf.

"Me too," mumbled Angus. "Except that I'm hungry."

A sudden scuffling sound inside the cave startled the four. They turned toward the entrance in time to see the boulder roll back, blocking the mouth of the cave.

"Ha-ha!" Bilge and Maggot called from inside the cave. "You can't get in! It's our cave now!"

"Saint George's dragon!" exclaimed Lucinda. "Do they really think we can't budge that boulder?"

"Let them think so for a while, Lucy," said Ethelred. "It's peaceful here."

Lucinda nodded. "Let's have a nice hot cup of tea and figure out how to get rid of those pests."

Then to Wiglaf's surprise, Lucinda opened her big red purse and took out a teakettle. She trotted over to a nearby mountain stream and filled it with water.

Ethelred opened her big red purse, too. She took out a teapot, a drawstring bag, two teacups, and two saucers. She sprinkled some dried green leaves from the bag into the pot. "You never know when you're going to need a bracing cup of tea. Sit down on those rocks, lads. Make yourselves comfortable."

Lucinda blew red-hot flames at the kettle. The water inside quickly boiled. She poured it over the tea in the pot, let it steep, and filled two cups.

Lucinda handed Wiglaf and Angus cups and

saucers. "I hope you like dragonmint tea."

Wiglaf sipped the tea. "Mmmm," he said. "Tasty."

Angus took a gulp. "Excellent!" he said. "Like peppermint, but mintier."

The dragon ladies exchanged pleased smiles.

"Oh, I nearly forgot!" Ethelred opened her purse again and took out a big bag of cookies. She gave each lad two. "I suppose this will have to do for your supper."

"No problem!" said Angus. He quickly took a bite. His eyes lit up. "Yum!"

"Dragonmint chip," Lucinda said.

Wiglaf thought he had never tasted anything so delicious.

"Now," said Ethelred, taking back the cups and pouring tea for herself and her sister. "How shall we get rid of those nasty little cave snatchers?" Her orange eyes narrowed. "Most dragons would just flame them."

"Or fly them up high in the sky and drop them," said Ethelred, stirring her tea.

"Or claw them to bits," Lucinda added.

Wiglaf shuddered at the thought. He began to feel ill.

"Um...they *are* my little cousins," Angus reminded the dragons.

"Some dragons would sit on them and crush them," Ethelred said, seeming to ignore Angus's comment.

"Or cook them for supper," added Lucinda. "Though I think they would be quite tough."

Wiglaf put down his half-eaten cookie. "Is there not some way to make them leave your cave without hurting them?" he asked.

"What we're getting at," said Lucinda, "is that most dragons would simply off those boys. But Ethelred and I aren't most dragons."

Wiglaf was glad to hear her say so!

"Let's see..." Ethelred drummed her claws thoughtfully on her scaly red chin. "We could send them a dragon stink bomb. Nothing smells worse than dragon—"

"No, sister!" Ethelred cried. "We'd never get *that* smell out of the cave."

"Well, how about inviting the family over?" said Lucinda. "The sight of 376 dragons would scare off those little hooligans."

"Don't count on it," said Angus.

"Plus, we'd have to feed all 376," said Ethelred. "And they might stay on for weeks."

"Scratch that idea," said Lucinda.

They all thought in silence for a while.

At last Wiglaf spoke up. "At Dragon Slayers' Academy, we learn—"

"*That's* where you go to school?" cried Ethelred.

"Oops!" Wiglaf put a hand over his mouth.

"Honestly, Ethelred!" Lucinda shook her head. "Where did you think they went to school? Princess Prep? Go on, Wiglaf."

"That—that all dragons have hoards of gold,"

Wiglaf managed.

Lucinda nodded. "It's true. My sister and I have a huge hoard. What about it?"

"If you were willing to part with some of your gold," said Wiglaf, "I think I know how you could get rid of Bilge and Maggot."

"We're all ears," said Ethelred. She wiggled hers.

"Bilge and Maggot wrote a fake ransom note to Headmaster Mordred," Wiglaf said. "They asked him to send a wheelbarrow piled high with gold."

"But Uncle Mordred ripped up the note," Angus put in. "He loves gold more than anything. Even more than his own nephews."

"But if you offered to *give* Mordred gold," Wiglaf said, "he might come and take Bilge and Maggot."

"I see," said Lucinda. "You mean we'd pay him an un-ransom to come and get the little snipes."

Wiglaf nodded.

Ethelred sighed. "As a rule, a dragon's hoarding instinct is very strong—especially in dragons from fine old families like ours."

"Parting with our gold," said Lucinda, "well, it just isn't done."

"No," said Ethelred. "Never."

The dragon sisters exchanged looks.

"However," Lucinda said slowly, "perhaps we could make an exception—this one time."

"We might give up some of our gold," added Ethelred, "if it would get rid of those hooligans."

Lucinda pawed around in her big red purse and found a piece of parchment.

Ethelred searched her purse and came up with a tin of ink and a large quill. "I will be the un-ransom–note secretary. What shall I say?"

"Dear Headmaster Mordred," began Wiglaf.

"Flatter him more," said Lucinda.

Wiglaf grinned. Lucinda had never met Mordred, yet she understood him perfectly.

In the end Ethelred wrote the following un-ransom note:

Esteemed Headmaster of DSA:

We are writing to let you know about a once-in-a-lifetime get-rich-quick opportunity. If you will come to our cave and fetch two lads who got lost on their way to your school—and guarantee that these lads, known as Bilge and Maggot, will never at any time ever return to our cave—we will give you a wheelbarrow piled high with gold. Send a reply as soon as possible.

Most sincerely,

Lucinda and Ethelred von Arnazmertz

Keep Away Mountain Cave

Ethelred proofread the un-ransom note. "Not one spelling mistake." She smiled. "What's the best way to get this to Mordred?"

"You could fly it to the school," suggested Wiglaf.

"*To Dragon Slayers' Academy?*" said Lucinda. "Not smart."

"Don't worry," said Angus. "My uncle Mordred is way too cheap to hire guards. If you deliver the note in the dark, no one will see you."

"Leave it on the drawbridge, under a rock," said Wiglaf. "That's where Mordred's scout, Yorick, found the other note."

Ethelred folded the note and tucked it into her big red purse.

"Dragon Slayers' Academy is just off Hunts-man's Path, right?" she asked.

"Right," said Angus.

Ethelred smiled. "This un-ransom note is as good as delivered."

Chapter 9

 short time later Ethelred returned. "Mission accomplished," she said.

"Oh, goodie!" exclaimed Lucinda. "I wonder when we shall get a reply?"

"Not for a while," said Angus. "It took us a long time to hike up here."

"Let's play a game to pass the time," said Lucinda. "Do you lads know how to play charades?"

Angus nodded. But Wiglaf shook his head.

"Twenty questions?" said Lucinda.

Wiglaf shook his head again. "The only game my family ever plays is Go Belch."

"Oh!" Lucinda put a paw to her mouth and giggled.

"Maybe these lads would like to see our Fire-Breather Follies act, sister," Ethelred said.

Lucinda smiled. "Eth and I were quite the rage when we were young."

"You were singers?" asked Wiglaf.

"And dancers!" said Lucinda. "Oh, those were the days! Shall we, sister?"

The dragons hopped up. They put their arms around each other's waists and began to sing:

Some dragons love a good brawl,
Looting and pillage don't thrill us at all,
We just are not that sort of girls,
We'd rather dress up—in our pearls.

The dragons let go of each other and did a little dance. Then they sang:

Some dragons flame night and day,
That's not how we like to play,

We like to rumba and cha-cha and—hey, watch us twirl!

We'd much rather dance—in our pearls.

Here the dragon sisters spun around and did some fancy footwork.

"Yay!" cried Wiglaf and Angus when the act ended. They clapped and cheered.

"Thank you," said Lucinda. She and Ethelred bowed.

"Next, we'll sing, 'Tea for Two,' " said Ethelred. "Ready?"

The dragon sisters began singing and dancing again.

Wiglaf had never known such talented dragons. He and Angus enjoyed the act enormously.

And yet, when the dragon sisters began singing their fifteenth song, Wiglaf began to wonder how many more songs they might sing. He glanced at Angus and saw that he was dozing. He elbowed him. It would not do to let the dragon ladies know that they were bored.

The show went on. And on and on. It might have gone on much longer, except that as the dragon ladies took a bow after their twenty-sixth song, Ethelred squinted into the distance. "Look, Lucy!" she asked. Someone is hiking up to our cave!"

Sure enough, way down the mountain, Wiglaf saw a gray-clad figure hurrying their way.

"It's our reply!" Ethelred squealed. "I just know it!"

Wiglaf and Angus ran down the mountain path, calling, "Yorick! Yorick!"

"Bless my stockings!" Yorick exclaimed when they reached him. "What in the name of mildew pudding are you lads doing up here?"

"'Tis a long story," said Wiglaf. He saw that Yorick was wearing his rock disguise: a gray hooded tunic, gray leggings, and gray boots. In this outfit he could hide in plain sight by crouching down by the side of the road. Passersby would see only a big, gray rock.

"Come meet the dragons, Yorick," said Angus.

Yorick stopped on the spot. "My ears must be clogged," he said. "I thought you said meet the dragons."

"I did." Angus nodded.

"They are very kind dragon ladies," Wiglaf put in.

"Oh, by my itchy feet, I won't be meeting any dragons," said Yorick.

"Yoo-hoo!" called Ethelred. "Are you Mordred's messenger?"

Yorick took one look at the huge, red-scaled dragon trotting down the mountain toward him, and hit the dirt. He doubled himself up small, pretending to be a rock.

"Where is the messenger?" Ethelred asked

when she reached them. "Where is our reply?"

An arm holding a parchment scroll sprang from the rock. Ethelred plucked the scroll out of Yorick's hand.

"Message delivered, my dragoness!" Yorick said, his voice muffled by his head being tucked under his belly.

Lucinda joined her sister on the path. Ethelred stuck a claw under the sealing wax on the scroll and popped it open. She read the message out loud:

Honored Dragons:

I will take Bilge and Maggot off your hands. But one wheelbarrow piled high with gold? Ladies, ladies! The lads are twins. It is only fair that you send me twin wheelbarrows piled high with gold— nothing less will do.

If you agree, send word with my scout, and I shall meet you midnight tonight by the Stunted Oak on Huntsman's Path. (It would not do for

the headmaster of DSA to be seen consorting with
dragons on campus.) You bring the gold. I'll bring
the wheelbarrows.

> *Eagerly awaiting,*
> *Mordred de Marvelous,*
> *Headmaster, DSA*
> *P.S. They are extremely large wheelbarrows.*

"Good heavens!" exclaimed Lucinda. "He is greedy!" She turned to Ethelred.

"He wants double the gold."

A crash sounded from deep inside the cave.

"Let's do it, Lucy," said Ethelred. "Peace and quiet are priceless."

"Scout?" Lucinda nudged Yorick the Rock with her foot. "Are you in there?"

"I am, my dragoness!" came the muffled reply.

"Tell Mordred we'll be at the Stunted Oak at midnight," said Lucinda. "With the gold."

"I shall, my dragoness!" said Yorick.

"Farewell!"

Wiglaf watched, amazed, as Yorick the Rock teetered back and forth, then began to roll. Down the mountain he went, picking up speed as he rolled. Soon he rolled out of sight.

"Alas, poor Yorick," said Wiglaf.

Angus shook his head. "Who knew he was so scared of dragons?"

Lucinda beamed at Wiglaf and Angus. "Your idea is working!"

"Come, sister," Ethelred said. "We must hurry to our storage cave to fetch our gold. We haven't much time."

"Be right back, lads," Lucinda said. She and her sister disappeared over a hill.

Angus glanced at Wiglaf's half-eaten cookie. "Are you going to eat that?"

Wiglaf shoved the cookie toward him.

Angus took a big bite. "Mmmm. I wonder if Lucinda will give me the recipe."

When Lucinda and Ethelred returned, each

was carrying a bulging sack.

"We'll fly you lads to Huntsman's Path," offered Lucinda.

"We get to ride on your backs?" cried Angus. "Oh, boy! Whoopie!"

Wiglaf smiled weakly. He wasn't fond of flying. Heights made him feel dizzy.

"I'll take you, Angus," said Ethelred.

"Hop on, Wiglaf," said Lucinda. She squatted down beside him.

Wiglaf stretched up and grabbed hold of Lucinda's knobby spine. He was about to pull himself onto her back when he heard shouting coming from inside the cave.

The dragons and lads stared as the boulder rolled back slightly from the entrance. Bilge and Maggot darted out of the cave, their armor clattering loudly.

"We want a ride on a dragon's back!" shouted Bilge.

"Yeah!" shouted Maggot. "Take us for a

ride! We want to go flying!"

Ethelred and Lucinda exchanged glances.

"Do you promise to stay out of our cave?" asked Lucinda.

"Forever?" said Ethelred.

"Promise!" shouted Bilge. "We're sick of that old cave."

"Yeah!" said Maggot. "Just take us on a ride!"

"Hop on!" said Ethelred. She lowered herself so they could.

The twins dug their grubby fingers in between Ethelred's scales and climbed up onto her back.

"Giddyap!" cried Bilge.

"Yeah!" cried Maggot. "Give us a crazy ride!"

"You asked for it," said Ethelred.

Safe on the ground below, Wiglaf watched Ethelred soar up into the air. She arched her back and turned a midair backward somersault.

"Aaaaaahhhh!" screamed the twins, who were dangling from her back.

Next, Ethelred did a perfect forward layout loop-the-loop. Then she tucked her head for a triple-lutz spin, followed by a double flip with a half twist.

"Aaaaaahhhh!" screamed the twins, twice as loud as before.

"I'm gonna be sick!" screamed a twin. But they were too far up in the air now for Wiglaf to tell which twin was screaming.

"You two can ride with me," Lucinda said, waggling a claw at Wiglaf and Angus.

Wiglaf's heart beat fast as he climbed onto Lucinda's back. He threw his arms around her red scaly neck. Angus climbed up behind Wiglaf and held on to Wiglaf's waist.

"Ready?" said Lucinda. She unfurled her great red wings and began flapping. She rose quickly into the air. Wiglaf tightened his grip on her neck.

Lucinda tilted midair, turning away from Keep Away Mountain and toward the valley below.

Wiglaf slowly relaxed. He began to enjoy the feeling of soaring through the full-moon night on the back of a dragon. The only sounds he heard were the flapping of wings. And somewhere high above in the black sky, the twins shrieking their heads off.

Chapter 10

From high upon the dragon's back, Wiglaf spotted the Stunted Oak below. Mordred leaned against the twisted tree trunk. The headmaster wore his red velvet cloak and cap. Beside him on the path stood two giant wheelbarrows.

"Halloooo!" Mordred called. He waved up at Lucinda. "Try for a nice soft landing. No bump! We wouldn't want any of the you-know-what to spill out!"

Wiglaf felt only a small jolt as Lucinda touched down. He and Angus slid off her back.

"Egad!" exclaimed Mordred, eyeing them. "Nephew! Wiglaf! What are you two doing here? The dragons didn't give *you* any of my gold, did they?"

"Fear not, Uncle," said Angus. "Your gold is safe."

"Here it is, Mordred," said Lucinda. She swung the sack off her back, opened it, and poured. Gold coins clattered into a waiting wheelbarrow.

"Oh! Oh!" cried Mordred. "Music to my ears!" He quickly snatched a coin and bit down on it. "Ow! Nearly cracked a molar." He grinned. "It's real gold, all right! What? Is the bag empty already? You call that heaping?"

"I do," said Lucinda, eyeing Mordred firmly. "This wheelbarrow is full."

"Well, how about the other one?" Mordred said. "We made a deal for two, you know."

Lucinda glanced up. "Here comes my sister now," she said, pointing a claw at a tiny speck in the night sky. "She has the other bag of gold."

Wiglaf heard the twins shrieking as Ethelred circled twice overhead. Flying in low, she did a last quadruple flip.

"Noooooo!" screamed the twins.

Ethelred landed with a bump on Huntsman's Path. "Ride over," she said.

Bilge and Maggot melted off the dragon's back. They staggered a few dizzy steps and fell to the ground. In the moonlight Wiglaf saw that their faces had turned a sickly green.

"We brought you the gold and the twins, too," said Ethelred.

"Hallo, Uncle," said Bilge from where he lay on the ground. "We rode here on the back of a dragon."

"The dragon did flips in the air," said Maggot as he rose to a wobbly stand. "Can we do it again, dragon? Can we? Can we?"

"You mean you *liked* it?" exclaimed Wiglaf.

"Yeah," said Maggot. "It was awesome."

"Enough!" said Mordred. "Back to business."

"Back to business!" Bilge mimicked.

"Button it up!" Mordred boomed.

"Button it up!" taunted the twins.

The twins burst out laughing.

Mordred glared at the pair. He turned to the dragons. "What about my second wheelbarrow of gold?"

"Here you go," said Ethelred. She poured her bag of gold into the empty wheelbarrow.

Mordred sank his arms into the huge pile of gold coins and hugged them tightly. "My gold," he crooned. "All mine."

"Only," said Lucinda, "if you keep Bilge and Maggot away from our cave."

"Don't worry about them," said Mordred. "My school is known for turning worthless lads into fine young dragon sla—I mean, fine young men. Bilge and Maggot won't be bothering you again. I'll whip them into shape in no time."

"Wanna bet?" said Angus softly.

"Farewell, Wiglaf," said Lucinda. "Farewell, Angus. I wish you could visit us again. But I'm going to booby-trap the path up to our cave." She shrugged. "Sorry, but no one without wings will ever pop in on us unexpectedly again."

"Thanks for the cookies," said Angus.

"We want another ride, dragon!" demanded Bilge.

"Yeah!" said Maggot. "Give us another crazy ride!"

But the dragon twins ignored them. They spread their wings and flew off toward their cave on Keep Away Mountain.

"Well!" Mordred rubbed his hands together. "Let's get my loot back to DSA. Nephew? You push that wheelbarrow. Wiglaf? You push this one. Nice and smooth now. Can't have coins dropping out. Hmm. I wonder if I'm going to need a bigger safe."

Angus and Wiglaf grabbed the wheelbarrow handles. By gritting their teeth and pushing with all their might, they made the wheels turn. They pushed the giant wheelbarrows down Huntsman's Path.

"Bilge?" called Mordred. "Maggot? You walk behind. Pick up any spillage. I have my eye on you. If I see you slipping coins into your pockets, I'll turn you upside down and shake them out."

The twins skipped along behind the huge wheelbarrows.

"We must get back to DSA before dawn," said Mordred, bringing up the rear. "Won't do to have students and teachers waking up and seeing all this gold." He cupped his hands to his mouth and called, "Put on a little speed, nephew! You too, Wiglaf. Pick up the pace."

It wasn't easy to push the wobbly, fully loaded wheelbarrows at any speed. But Wiglaf and Angus did their best to go faster.

The sky was pink with dawn when Wiglaf spotted DSA in the distance.

Not far from the drawbridge, Angus stopped. "I...can't...push...more," he panted.

Wiglaf stopped, too. He had never been so tired.

"We'll help you!" called Bilge. He grabbed the handles of the wheelbarrow Angus had been pushing.

"Yeah," said Maggot, grabbing the handles of Wiglaf's barrow. "We'll help!"

Angus and Wiglaf dropped onto the grass, exhausted.

The little lads shoved hard and managed to get the wheels rolling. Bilge pushed his wheelbarrow up onto the drawbridge. Maggot was right behind.

"They are strong for such little lads," said Wiglaf, watching them.

"Careful now, lads," Mordred called, hurrying toward the drawbridge. "Keep 'em steady. Don't want any coins spilling into the moat."

Hearing this, the twins looked at each other and grinned. Then they started wobbling the wheelbarrows from side to side on the bridge.

"Ooooh!" cried Bilge. "This is heavy!"

"Yeah!" cried Maggot. "It's gonna tip over!"

Wiglaf gasped. "They're doing it on purpose!"

"Careful!" shrieked Mordred, galloping toward the bridge. "Stop! Stop!"

But the twins did not stop. They wobbled the giant barrows crazily from one side of the bridge to the other.

Mordred leaped onto the bridge. His face was eggplant purple. His violet eyes gleamed with rage. "STOP!" he boomed. "LET GO OF MY WHEELBARROWS!"

"All right, Uncle!" said Bilge. He raised his hands from the rolling barrow.

Mordred lunged at Bilge's barrow. But he was too late. It bumped over the side of the bridge and plunged into the moat. Piled high with gold as it was, it sank quickly to the bottom—if there was a bottom—of the moat.

Mordred clawed at his face in horror. "What have you done?" he shrieked.

"This, Uncle," said Maggot. "He did THIS." And he gave his wheelbarrow a shove.

"NOOOOOOOOOOOOOOOOOOOOO!" screamed Mordred as the second wheelbarrow splashed into the moat and—BLOOP!—vanished.

"I'll save you, my poor gold!" Mordred cried as he leaped into the moat. SPLASH! He disappeared under the murky waters.

"Alas, poor Uncle Mordred," said Angus.

"Bilge and Maggot are scary," said Wiglaf. "No wonder Mordred tore up that ransom note."

Mordred's head popped up in the moat. "Bilge!" he cried. "Maggot! Dive in and get my gold!"

"Fat chance!" shouted the little lads. They cracked up laughing.

Mordred's booted feet kicked up a splash as he dove down once more.

"Erica will be sad that she missed this adventure," said Angus.

"But she will be very happy with the big, exciting story we shall write for the *DSA News*," said Wiglaf.

"True," said Angus, as Mordred's head popped up in the moat once more. "We've got a front-page story for sure."

DSA NEWS

Written by students for students with absolutely no supervision!   *Vol. II*

WHO'S SCARIER— DRAGONS OR TWINS? YOU DECIDE

by Wiglaf of Pinwick

In a deep dark cave Angus and I were held prisoners. But it was not dragons that trapped us. It was Angus's twin cousins, Bilge and Maggot.

They wrecked the cave that was the retirement home of two lady dragons named Lucinda and Ethelred. When these dragons get upset, their crests pop up on their heads, their eyes shoot sparks, and their pearls glow like red-hot lava. They are VERY scary. But in truth, they are not half as scary as Bilge and Maggot.

Bilge and Maggot are DSA's newest students. Maybe if we are nice to them, they will behave. It's worth a try!

STASH SAVES THE DAY!

by Angus du Pangus

There we were at the bottom of a deep pit. Things looked hopeless for Wiglaf and me.

Then I remembered my stash of goodies. Wiglaf and I began eating Jolly Jelly Worms. Bilge and Maggot were watching us, and I could tell they were getting hungry. So I got out Graham Cookies, Medieval Marshmallows, and Cocoa Cubes. That did it. Bilge and Maggot threw us a rope, and we climbed out of the pit.

What did I learn from this experience?

Two things:

It is good to carry a little stash with you at all times.

It is bad to be related to Bilge and Maggot.

GET TO KNOW ME!

by Gwendolyn of Gargglethorp

Royal greetings to all! My parents rule Gargglethorp. That makes me a princess—duh! I am very good at getting my own way. Practically everything I have is made of gold: my hairbrush, even my toothbrush! I went to Pretty Little Princess Preschool. Then I attended Princess Prep. I made all A's, but I got sick of taking classes like the Princess Walk and Princess Knitting. That's why I transferred to DSA. I love the new DSA lasses' uniforms. I am so into fashion, and read *Damsels' Wear Daily* like every single day! My closet is totally stuffed with clothes. (If you have any room in your dorm closet, let me know, will you?) Oh, and Wiglaf? How about sitting next to me in Slaying Class next week?

My Full Name is...
Princess Gwendolyn
Glorianna of Gargglethorp

My Favorite Subject is... Me!

My Favorite Food is...
Anything
served to me on a tray.

My Favorite Riddle is...
Why couldn't the princess skeleton go to the dance?
She had no *body* to go with!

COOKIN' WITH FRYPOT

by **Angus du Pangus**

A lovely dragon lady was kind enough to give me the recipe for a dragon-sized batch of dragonmint chip cookies. They're delicious and easy to bake—adjust cooking methods when necessary. Bon appétit!

DRAGONMINT CHIP COOKIES

Ingredients:

3 pawfuls wild dragonmint
6 pawfuls flour
$\frac{1}{8}$ pawful salt
7 pounds goose fat
2 pawfuls red hot sugar
4 pawfuls brown sugar
$\frac{1}{3}$ pawful vanilla
6 large goose eggs

Chop dragonmint until it forms a sticky paste. Roll into balls. Cut each ball into quarters to make chips. Set aside.

Combine flour and salt in a bowl. Set aside.

Cream together lard, red-hot sugar, brown sugar, vanilla, and goose eggs.

Add flour mixture to goose fat. Toss in dragonmint chips. Stir. Place batter on cookie sheet. Open your mouth and flame cookies until done. Enjoy!

ASK ERICA

Advice from Erica von Royale

Dear Erica,
I bet your readers would like to read an article in DSA NEWS about a town that's an easy walk from school. I'm talking about Toenail Village, just three rodlongs north of DSA on Huntsman's Path.
            A Lad from Toenail

Dear Lad,
      DSA NEWS is a school paper. We don't do articles on nearby villages. Why don't you pick a school-related topic?

Dear Erica,
I could write about Toenail's great shopping. And how you can buy pies at Jack's Bake Shop, have your shoes mended at Jack's Cobblery, and get your wheels fixed at Jack's Wagon Garage.
            A Lad from Toenail

Dear Lad,
      Can't you take no for an answer?

Dear Erica,
Or I could write about the great theater in Toenail. And how you can bring your own rotten eggs and spoiled tomatoes to throw at the actors. Or you can buy them in the lobby.
            A Lad from Toenail

Dear Lad,
      Give it up!

Dear Erica,
I could also write about the fine dining in Toenail. It's all-you-can-eat night every night at Wild Boar Willy's. If sitting on boards, grabbing food, and sloshing ale isn't your scene, try Tess's Tea Shoppe.
            A Lad from Toenail

Dear Lad,
      As editor-in-chief of the DSA NEWS, I have the right say what goes into this paper. There will be no stories about Toenail.
      Ever.

Dear Erica,
Ha-ha! There just was.
            A Lad from Toenail

*** Have a question for Erica? Write to her in care of the *DSA News*!***

The DSA Sports Report

by Charley Marley

Frypot said his ox did not want to be the DSA Jousting team's steed anymore.

After that, everybody quit the team.

THE END

Help Wanted

LIBRARY ASSISTANT

Dost thou knowest thine alphabet from A to Z? Dost thou likest to worketh with books? Wouldst thou liketh to be paid in peanut brittle?

If thou answereth YES to these questions, cometh up to the library and chatteth with Brother Dave about a job as a Book Shelver.

Contact:
Brother Dave

GOOD DEEP DIVER

Looking for lad or lass who wants to earn extra pocket change in exchange for diving into the DSA moat to look for...something. Only lads or lasses who can keep a secret need apply.

Contact:
Headmaster Mordred, DSA

Overheard in...
SIR MORT'S CLASSROOM
by Baldrick de Bold

As this reporter snuck into Sir Mort's class late, he heard lads and lasses saying:

"Is Sir Mort awake?"

"Poke him and see."

"You poke him."

"No, you."

"No, you."

"Is he dead?"

"Maybe."

"I don't think he's breathing."

"Then who's that snoring?"

Frypot's eels make your belly ache?
Come to Smilin's Hal's for some fried dough and a shake!

I Penny off last week's clams!

Smilin' Hal's
Off-Campus Eatery

Think Frypot's eels might be tainted? Head for Smilin' Hal's—it's just been painted!

Smilin' Hal's
Off-Campus Eatery

Local Restaurant to Close

by Angus du Pangus

A health inspector visited Smilin' Hal's Off-Campus Eatery last week and threatened to close the place down. He cited it for 1,027 health violations, and that was before he set foot in the kitchen.

Other diners there at the time say that the inspector took Smilin' Hal up on his offer of a free lunch, and his gut cramped up so fast that he could not finish his report.

"Come on down!" says Smilin' Hal. "We're not closed yet!"

DSA NEWS

Editor-in-Chief
ERICA VON ROYALE

Reporters:

Lifestyle and Food:

ANGUS DU PANGUS

Book Reviews: BRAGWORT

Sports Beat: CHARLIE MARLEY

General Reporting:

JANICE SMOTHERBOTTOM

WIGLAF OF PINWICK

GWEN OF GARGGLETHORP

BALDRICK DE BOLD

Faculty Advisor: SIR MORT